Ronda AND THE Garden OF THE Gulf

by J. Dunham • illustrated by William Low

Orlando   Boston   Dallas   Chicago   San Diego

Visit *The Learning Site!*
www.harcourtschool.com

Hello, my name is Ronda Pasquale, and today my teacher, Mrs. Rodriguez, is taking our sixth-grade class on a field trip all the way from our home in northern Maine to Prince Edward Island in Canada! I'm keeping a record of everything that happens in my science journal, and I'm so excited I can hardly wait!

5:30 A.M.—About to leave for our trip

It's time to get up and drive to the airport. My father is driving me, and once we get there we'll meet up with Mrs. Rodriguez and the rest of my classmates. Today my father will be one of Mrs. Rodriguez's helpers (to make sure that nobody gets lost or does anything goofy).

AIRPORT 10 miles

6:30 A.M.—At the airport

It's autumn right now. The weather in Maine is starting to cool down, and all of my friends have brought extra sweaters just in case it gets very, very cold on Prince Edward Island, where, at this time of year, the temperature can fluctuate anywhere from the mid-40s to 70 degrees Fahrenheit. Mrs. Rodriguez warned us to bring plenty of winter stuff because even if it's warm during the day, it cools off at night.

If you want to know why, I can tell you (because Mrs. Rodriguez taught us all about factors that affect temperature). You see, Prince Edward Island is located off the mainland of Canada and is surrounded by a large body of water called the Gulf of St. Lawrence. The gulf waters help the island remain temperate, meaning the temperature is usually warmer there than in the rest of Canada. It's also wetter on Prince Edward Island because the island gets a lot of rain—due to the water that surrounds it. (In case you were wondering, large bodies of water create clouds, which then make rain, especially when it's warm. In other words, if you live near a large body of water, you should expect a climate with heavy rainfall and milder temperatures.)

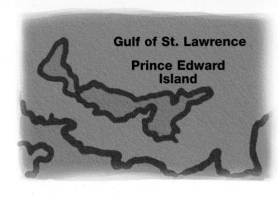

Gulf of St. Lawrence

Prince Edward Island

9:00 A.M.—In Canada, yes!!

Well, after a remarkably short plane ride, we have arrived safely in Canada! It seems strange that the trip was so short, and yet we're in a completely different country.

Mrs. Rodriguez says that we could have flown all the way to Prince Edward Island (called "PEI" for short), but she wanted to show us something special, as a treat, on the way. My dad says that he knows what the treat is, but his lips are sealed.

9:30 A.M.—On the way to PEI—wow!

We're crossing Confederation Bridge, the biggest bridge I've ever seen (it's thirteen kilometers, or about eight miles long). It is, by the way, what Mrs. Rodriguez selected as our special treat.

Looking out the bus window, I can see water stretching out all around us, and it's one of the most dramatically beautiful sights I've ever seen in my life. I also notice some boats, some birds, and I think I can even see some jumping fish!

4

As we get near PEI, I'm beginning to understand why people call this island the "Garden of the Gulf." It's beautiful and green with amazing amounts of vegetation; seeing it makes me want to hop off this bus to take a look around!

10:00 A.M.—PEI, at last!!

We have finally arrived on PEI, which has a curved shape (kind of like a smile), as Mrs. Rodriguez already explained to us. She says that this place, the Garden of the Gulf, is known for its rich agriculture. In fact, its red soil, temperate climate, and moist environment are perfect for growing potatoes. Farmers also grow other types of vegetables here, and they raise chickens, hogs, and cows, as well.

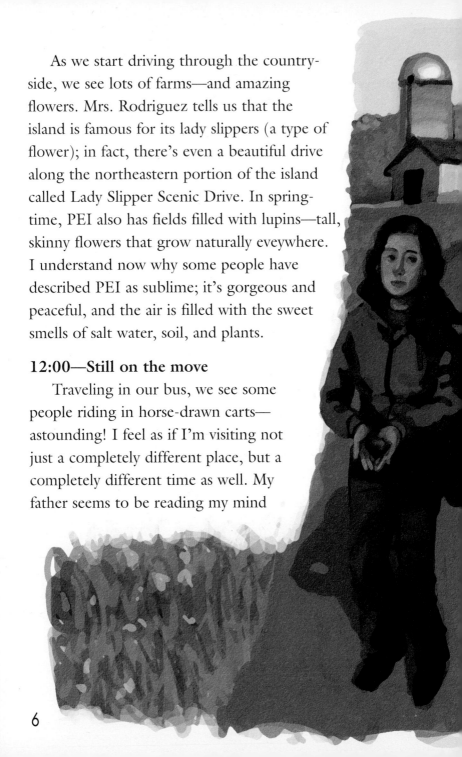

As we start driving through the country-side, we see lots of farms—and amazing flowers. Mrs. Rodriguez tells us that the island is famous for its lady slippers (a type of flower); in fact, there's even a beautiful drive along the northeastern portion of the island called Lady Slipper Scenic Drive. In spring-time, PEI also has fields filled with lupins—tall, skinny flowers that grow naturally eveywhere. I understand now why some people have described PEI as sublime; it's gorgeous and peaceful, and the air is filled with the sweet smells of salt water, soil, and plants.

12:00—Still on the move

Traveling in our bus, we see some people riding in horse-drawn carts—astounding! I feel as if I'm visiting not just a completely different place, but a completely different time as well. My father seems to be reading my mind

when he tells me, "It's as if we've taken a time capsule back to a simpler, gentler age."

Then he teases me and asks whether I'm ready to pack up all our belongings and move here with Mom, because he's already in love with PEI. When he says those words, I don't even laugh because I think I'm in love with it, too.

Because it's autumn, we get to see a rainbow of colors in the trees—orange, yellow, and red. Mrs. Rodriguez reminds us that soon the leaves will turn brown and fall, as the trees enter their dormant season—the cold winter months.

One problem on PEI, she explains, is that freezing rain, or sleet, sometimes damages the trees in winter. This seems quite logical, when I think about it, because PEI is located at a high latitude, up north where the temperatures can get quite cold. As far as I can see, though, the plant life is doing quite well here; in fact, the island is filled with growing things—not just plants teeming everywhere you look, but lots and lots of animals scampering around in the plants as well.

1:00 P.M.—Lunch break

At last we stop to eat lunch, and I'm starving! We are at Prince Edward Island National Park on Cavendish Beach, and it is beautiful. It's huge, there's sand all over the place, and it has reddish dunes and cliffs far back from the water's edge. Even though we're all hungry—starving, in fact—it's simply irresistible to run around and take a closer look, so we do exactly that. Of course, we've been warned to stay close to our group, and we're always careful to obey that rule, but we enjoy getting a closer look at these strange dunes.

8

Later, while we're munching on sandwiches and apples, Mrs. Rodriguez points to a funny-looking bird with a long, skinny beak; a white head; and a gray-blue body. (I bet this coloring acts as camouflage against the gray-blue water, to hide it from other animals that might get ideas about using it for food.)

The most remarkable characteristic of this unusual bird (to me, at least) is that it stands almost four feet high—almost as tall as I am! Mrs. Rodriguez explains that it is a great blue heron.

Mrs. Rodriguez tells us that great blue herons love PEI because they find lots of fish and immense stretches of quiet water there (where there aren't many waves or other animals, especially people). The great blue herons have long legs that help them fish. They stand very quietly in the water, almost statuelike, and wait for their prey to swim past; then, in an instant, they plunge their heads down into the water to scoop a fish into their mouths.

Right now the herons are getting ready to migrate from the island because of the frigid cold of the coming winter, but since early spring they have lived on PEI, nesting in groups called colonies. The herons take good care of their young, building them nests of sticks and twigs and protecting them high above the ground in trees. Sometimes the colonies grow to as many as 74 nests!

Mrs. Rodriguez explains that she'd been hoping we'd get a chance to see another interesting bird called the piping plover. Unfortunately, it's uncommon to spot the bird at this time of year, and, as Mrs. Rodriguez solemnly explained to us, the piping plover is on Canada's endangered species list. In other words, unless people make an effort to ensure its survival, the piping plover might soon become extinct.

The piping plover is a far smaller bird than the great blue heron; it measures only about 7 inches, but it has a wingspan about twice that length. Plovers eat insects, worms, mollusks, and other small beach creatures. They usually make their nests in early spring near the sand dunes of PEI. The males scrape a hole in the sand and convert it into a nest by lining it with stones and shells. (Ouch—that doesn't sound very comfortable to me!) After about a month, the baby birds hatch, and actually begin walking around within hours of their birth! By this time of year, Mrs. Rodriguez explains, the young have grown up and learned to fly, and all the plovers have flown to warmer places for the winter.

Just as we're getting ready to leave Cavendish Beach, we see something else exciting—a red fox! The beautiful animal runs when it sees us, but we are glad to have caught a glimpse of it. Mrs. Rodriguez explains that at one time silver foxes also raised families on Prince Edward Island.

3:30 P.M.—On the road again

We're back on the bus and on our way to a fishing port. Mrs. Rodriguez explains that in addition to being farmers, the people of PEI make their livelihood by fishing.

When we arrive at the docks of the port, we see lots of fishing boats bringing in their catch of the day or week. The fishermen are unloading an amazing variety of seafood —mackerel, tuna, flounder, oysters, and even lobsters!

5:30 P.M.—Hungry again

Mrs. Rodriguez has arranged for us to eat with some local citizens—what a treat! The islanders are so friendly, and they tell us how much they love living on PEI. They say they enjoy the temperate climate and the fresh ocean breezes; best of all, no place on the island is very far from a beach.

The people here take a great deal of pride in their island, and they work together to keep it clean and unspoiled. We all agree that PEI is spectacular and that it must be a pleasure to call the island home.

For our meal the people serve us lobster, home-baked bread, and fresh vegetables. They also offer us a delicious salad and many different kinds of desserts. When I tell one of our hostesses that, because our homes are far from the coast, lobster is such an amazing, gigantic treat for us, she looks bewildered, and then she chuckles. She explains, first of all, that we are very special guests to her, and second, that here on PEI they always eat lobster because lobster is plentiful in this lovely land by the sea.

Another of our hosts points out the window at a lighthouse in the distance and explains why lighthouses are extremely important to the island. Since fog frequently surrounds PEI, it's not unusual for a ship to get lost or crash into the shore during a storm. The lighthouses help sailors navigate around the island—especially during stormy weather. In the old days, lighthouse keepers had to keep careful watch to make sure the beacon was always shining for ships at sea, but today the lights are automatic.

Our host also tells a funny story about PEI's own potato museum. At first, my classmates and I giggle, and the man takes our laughter in good humor, but then he explains that it's true—the island does indeed have a potato museum. He explains that much of the island's economy depends on the potato, which grows so easily and naturally on PEI. He also tells us that if we ever get a chance to visit the museum, we'll see the world's biggest potato on display. We all look over at Mrs. Rodriguez (who's heard every word of our conversation), but she shakes her head sadly—no visit to the potato museum this trip, maybe another time.

Later we see the most beautiful sunset I've ever seen in my entire life—it's amazing! The sandstone cliffs above the beach glow red like fire, the sky turns gold and bronze, and I feel as if I am seeing something unique, something I will remember for the rest of my life. My father hands me my jacket, and I realize that I am a little chilled. I hadn't even noticed the cold before now because I've been concentrating on the sunset. I lean against my father and feel thrilled that he's here to share this wonderful moment with me.

7:30 P.M.—Farewell PEI

The warmer weather we experienced earlier in the day has turned into a chilly night, and everybody puts on more layers of clothing. We say good-bye to our hosts and hostesses and thank them for both a lovely meal and their wonderful conversation. We feel sad as we climb onto the bus. Many of us would like to stay longer, maybe to play on the beaches tomorrow; search for more blue herons, piping plovers, and red foxes; or enjoy the beauty of the woods and another glorious sunset.

Unfortunately, though, it is time for us to bid farewell to beautiful Prince Edward Island. As our bus drives back across the Confederation Bridge, I crane my neck to get one last glimpse of the lovely Garden of the Gulf. It truly is a glorious garden, filled with beauty in every nook and cranny: beautiful plants, wonderful animals, and amazing people.

9:00 P.M.—Home again

I am finally back home. My father has to shake me to wake me up when we stop in our driveway. My mother is waiting at the door as I come in, and I give her a big hug.

"I missed you both," she says. "How was it?"

I stand still for a moment, trying to think of words to describe Prince Edward Island. I start to get flustered because I'm afraid it's just not possible to get across what that astonishing island was really like. Finally, all I can say is, "It was beautiful—they call it the Garden of the Gulf, and now I think I understand why."